Forever in our hearts.

Until we meet again

Where are you?
Where are you?
Where did you go?

First of all, I would like to offer my condolences to all those
individuals who have lost a loved one.
May you find peace and comfort in your heart.
May you gradually learn to cope, adjust to your loss and
find the strength you need.

To my dear children Keila Renée A. and Bryan Christopher

A., with much love. I dedicate this book in memory of my

late husband René Alvizures

1966-2019.

A loving father, husband, friend, and happy soul.

Gone too soon.

As family, we unite to grieve as one,

but we truly suffer the pain on our own.

Acknowledgements

I would like to thank all of my FAMILY MEMBERS for being my support system during my time of grief. You know who you are.

To my ONLY TWO CHILDREN, I love you more than words can say, you are my life.

I thank GOD for giving me the daily strength that I need. For inspiring me to write this book and for giving me the peace and comfort that only he can provide.

I want to thank LIFE for clearly showing me that pain can either make or break you. It can teach you so many things about yourself that you didn't know before.

I thank RESILIENCY, for making me a stronger person and forcing me to channel all of my pain into something positive.

To my HUSBAND, who is no longer with me but whose love lives in my heart and soul, I would like to say "I love you BEYOND WORDS."

"Thank you for 34 years of friendship, companionship, marriage, love, happiness and life's lessons."

"You were a true blessing in my life, and you will always be the best husband in the world. The day you parted this world, it lost an amazing human, but thankfully the heavens gained an ANGEL."

I love you forever,

Your 80's GIRL

Where are you?
Where are you?
Where did you go?

Rocio M. Alvizures

Chapters

Chapter 1
Meet Rosie

There once was a girl named Rosie. She was a happy person until something life changing and sad happened to her. Someone close to her and who she loved very much passed away. It was her best friend. A friend that she spent all of her days with and the person who made her laugh so much.

Rosie cried so much because she missed that person very much. She knew that she would never see HIM again. That left her with feelings of sorrow and anger because she didn't think that going away forever was fair.

Rosie was confused and did not understand where that person went or why they had to go away. Every day she thought about how much she missed HIM. She often sat and wrote about how she felt in her journal and ended up with the following poem;

Where are you?

Where are you?

Where did you go?

We were together and had lots of fun,

if you ask me how much, I'd answer a ton!

One thing I know, I would see you a lot,

one day you're with me, the next day you're not.

I know that you passed and you had no choice,

but I miss your face and hearing your voice.

I know that you're far and beyond the sun,

but I wish there was something that I could have done.

I miss you a lot and it makes me sigh,

not having you near me is making me cry.

Each day has been rough and holidays too,

birthdays and outings remind me of you.

Saying goodbye, such a tough thing to do,

If you only knew; all the things I go through.

I hear you're in heaven and that you have your wings,

I hear that you fly and do all kinds of things.

I hear that you roam in a garden so green

and that it's like nothing that you've ever seen.

They say that one day, we will meet again

but until that happens, I ask myself when?

Not seeing your face and hearing your voice

is part of my life and I have no choice.

Where are you?

Where are you?

Where did you go?

Whenever I think of your smiling face,

it takes me away to a happy place.

A ladder to heaven, I wish could climb,

and stay right beside you all of the time.

I want you to squeeze me and to hold me tight

and tell me that everything will soon be alright.

One day while walking,

thought I heard you talking.

It was only the wind,

so I quickly grinned.

I want all the giggles,

I want all the laughter

and all of the fun that soon came right after.

I need you to stay; not only a day,

oh, why, oh, why, did you go away?

I look here, I look there,

I look around, but you're nowhere.

In the morning, noon and night,

I talk to you, it feels all right.

I search to find you everyday,

in the morning and mid-day.

Where are you?
Where are you?
Where did you go?

Chapter 2
Something amazing

As you already know, Rosie lost a loved one and is having a difficult time dealing with the loss. She continues to grieve and cry, but can't help feeling oh-so sad.

One warm afternoon, she sits down and decides to once again write in her journal. She wrote and wrote until late in the day.

She was a bit tired so, she stopped writing for a while and went for a walk. She suddenly found herself, walking down a path, which she had never been before. It led to a lush green garden. It was full of flowers and beautiful things. "What a wonderful place!" she said.

This place was such a peaceful and happy place. Rosie closed her eyes, took a deep breath, exhaled, and smiled.

Her walk continued, however little did Rosie know that she was about to enter a place where she would discover something incredible.

What happened next, took her by surprise, she couldn't believe it, and rubbed her eyes.

My goodness!
My goodness!
What's this I see?
Such beautiful sights right in front of me.

I see a SPARROW

passing by

and it was you, just flying high.

I see a lovely BUTTERFLY

there you are, just floating by.

I see a little LADYBUG,

thought of you and felt your hug.

I see the STARS that shine at night

and close my eyes so very tight.

I feel the closeness, just me and you,

oh, what a feeling, I sure miss you.

I see the CLOUDS and SKY so blue

I see you, see me too?

I see the WIND blow through a curtain,

it's a sign, of that I'm certain.

I see an orange DRAGONFLY,

I want to touch it, I think I'll try.

I see a furry BUMBLEBEE,

You're buzzing by to check on me.

I hear the sounds of soft WIND CHIMES,

and think of all our happy times.

I hear the beat to your FAVORITE SONG,

now nothing, nothing can go wrong.

I hear the sounds of the FALLING RAIN

And think of you again and again.

I hear the BIRDS that chirp and sing,

I think of you and it feels like spring.

I feel the BREEZE right on my face

it feels so good like your embrace.

I feel the warmth of the SUMMER SUN,

reminds me of the things we've done.

Rosie, wake up! Rosie, wake up!

She heard a voice from afar as someone was

calling her name. As she lifted her head from the

table where she was sleeping, she slowly opened

her eyes and asked "what is this?

What do you mean? Was this only but a

dream?" Yes, answered someone it was only a

dream. "That doesn't matter" she said, because

she was delighted.

Chapter 3
Before I forget

Even if it was a dream, it was a beautiful dream. All that mattered was that it felt surreal.

Every minute of that journey was a joyful moment.

She thought to herself, "Hmm, what if I could feel the same as I did in my dream, but while I am awake?" She was determined to see her loved as many times as possible.

Rosie grabbed her journal and made sure she wrote down everything that happened in her dream. She did it as quickly as she could before she would forget. And this is what she wrote;

In my dream I was with you,

was wide awake and heard you too.

I know that you're gone, no longer here

but you were with me, not far but near.

What a wonderful time I had with you,

I'm feeling real happy and no longer blue.

So pay close attention to every clue,

for what happened to me can happen to you.

There you were I couldn't believe it!

It was real, you came to visit.

I saw and heard you in different things,

I need you to know all the joy that it brings.

And now I ask, will I see you once more?

Of course I will and distance no more.

The key is to stop, listen and become more aware,

and finally realize that you're everywhere!

You're always with me and in my heart,

there's nothing on earth that could keep us apart.

Now I know, that thinking of you,

keeps your memory alive, so that's what I'll do.

My love for you fills my heart,

it's been like that right from the start.

One day I know, that I'll hold you tight,

and then I'll know that it's really alright.

So focused on sadness and missing you,

that my feelings of grief just grew and grew.

When someone's gone, tears fill your eyes,

but count the hellos and not the goodbyes.

Chapter 4
Change begins

Now I look for a sign or two,

because after your visit, I'm no longer blue.

All I do is stop and recall,

that your presence is with me and in pretty much all.

Being observant is all it takes,

now I can do it when I'm wide awake.

I smile more often; because of my dream,

gets me so excited, that I could just....scream!

Rosie's feelings of grief quickly began to turn into feelings of joy. She was able to turn all the sadness into happy thoughts and learned to smile while doing so.

She learned many things while on her journey. It showed her that those visits from her loved one could happen at any time. In her dream, she never felt alone because she was able to see her loved one in so many ways.

Rosie felt so happy because she could re-live her feelings of happiness just as she did in her dream. The difference was that she learned to do it while she was awake.

Meet Rosie and her best friend who passed away

Before her dream, she couldn't understand,

why he left her, it wasn't planned.

All she wanted was a longer stay,

instead of him leaving so far away.

All she knew was that he had gone,

and that there was nothing she could've done.

After her dream Rosie's pain had decreased,

in knowing her loved one was living in peace.

In a place where rainbows shine so bright,

the place where her loved one felt alright.

He lies on the clouds and catches some sun,

and then takes a stroll once he's finally done.

A place where rivers sparkle and glisten,

you could hear the trickling, if you'd only listen.

The hills and the valleys all covered with flowers,

it's a place he's enjoying and where he spends many hours.

Thanks to her dream, Rosie learned how to turn her feelings of sadness and grief into positive and joyous thoughts. You may be asking yourself, why was she was able to see her loved one in all the things she encountered in her dream?

It was because all those things that she saw made her happy, and seeing her loved one also made her happy. It was perfect! All of those things together, filled her up with such bliss.

Her dream made her realize that she was never alone. Her loved one was always with her. She discovered that yes, they left but went right into a place where they would never leave, inside her heart, mind, and soul.

Rosie was just happy with her dream and that she could see her loved one again. She learned that it was okay to miss someone and to sometimes feel sad but knew that she had to change that.

She did not want to remain in sadness and grief forever. Rosie wanted nothing more than to be happy and to smile once again.

So to help make you smile, this poem is for you,
if you are feeling sad and a little bit blue.
It was written to try and help you achieve,
some peace in your heart while you heal and grieve.

Chapter 5
Staying connected

If you ever lost a loved one and it could be anyone. Maybe it was a member of your family, a friend, a relative, a classmate, or pet. It doesn't matter who it was, losing someone special in your life hurts. One thing to do whenever you are having a rough day and your heart might be aching, is to let all of your feelings out with a good cry if necessary. Then after you are done, you can think of something positive for example; making happy memories. Think about it, you were given that person or pet in your life as part of a gift and blessing.

If you feel like you are alone, think again. You are never alone and all you have to do is to think of them and you won't be. You can always stay connected in so many ways and when you do, Rosie wants you to close your eyes just as she did and just think of the treasured times again and again. You can always feel free to talk to their picture or when you visit them in that place where they rest. You may not physically hear or see your loved one anymore but that doesn't mean your memory can't replay their voice and recall their face. Keep talking and thinking about them, and that way they will never be forgotten. Keep their memory alive! I'm sure they would really like that.

Now go ahead and look for things
that only memories might bring.
A stuffed animal, toy or a Christmas stocking.
A movie, a book or some pigeons flocking.

A certain song on the radio,
your favorite hits on the stereo.
The ocean waves, a quiet stream,
or songs on the truck that sells ice cream.

A birthday card, a letter or note,
a funny joke, or the words misspoke.
A bird that sings or flaps its wings,
it can practically be anything.

So when someone pays you a visit,

be sure you're ready so you won't miss it.

It sometimes will happen in interesting ways,

so just wait and see how all of it plays.

Whether it is in heaven, or any place you want them to be, there will always be a place for them. Just think of all the things they are doing. They might be playing, swimming, laughing, hearing beautiful music, and resting. They are alright and in good company. They have a lot of things to do in their new home. Be hopeful because one day in the future, you will see them again and you can continue doing all of the things that you used to do when you were together.

Chapter 6
A time for reflection

Time for reflection:

Read and answer the questions on the following pages.
After you finish, share your answers with a family
member or any adult that you choose. Talking about
your feelings is a helpful start in coping with your grief.
Try to open up and to share exactly how you feel.
It will make you feel better by letting things out.

Reading this book made me think of (insert name of loved one) because:

_____
_____
_____
_____
_____
_____
_____
_____
_____
_____
_____
_____
_____
_____
_____
_____
_____
_____
_____
_____
_____
_____
_____
_____
_____

I will do the following things to honor

(insert the name of a loved one)

and to keep their memory alive:

_____

_____

_____

_____

_____

_____

_____

_____

_____

_____

_____

_____

_____

_____

_____

_____

_____

_____

_____

_____

_____

_____

_____

I really miss (insert name of loved one) because:

_____

_____

_____

_____

_____

_____

_____

_____

_____

_____

_____

The following things remind me of

(insert name of a loved one)

_____

_____

_____

_____

_____

_____

_____

_____

_____

_____

_____

_____

Remember that losing someone can be a traumatic and tragic experience that may often feel like it is taking a toll on you. It might feel like that from time to time, but these feelings will decrease as time goes by. Grief is not easy, but you are truly stronger than you know or think. Please know that the way you feel matters to many people in your life. You may not think that talking matters or that nobody will understand you, but they will.

Make sure to communicate with others just exactly how you feel. You will be surprised how much better things can be once you let things out. The grief journey is one that you cannot go through by yourself. There will be many moments when you will not have people around you and you will cry. The pain you experience might seem unbearable from time to time, but just know that this is a natural part of grief process. You are mourning the loss of a loved one, so don't go through this on your own, talk to someone.

You might feel like you're alone, but you are not. You can start by saying "Can I talk to you?" and someone will be ready to listen. The people you can talk to are; parents, family members, friends, teachers, a school counselor, psychologist or a nurse. Once again, you are not alone in this nor should you feel like you are. There are people who care about you and the way you feel.

Now it's time to listen to Rosie's advice "when a butterfly, ladybug, or anything else visits you, make sure you close your eyes, think happy memories, open your eyes and then put a smile on your face."

Dear René, I will love you forever.

Always have and always will.

1985-Eternity.

www.ingramcontent.com/pod-product-compliance
Lightning Source LLC
Chambersburg PA
CBHW041149250626
47164CB00015B/187